This book
belongs to:

··································

Baa!

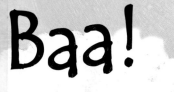

To Ste X

OXFORD
UNIVERSITY PRESS

Great Clarendon Street, Oxford OX2 6DP

Oxford University Press is a department of the University of Oxford.
It furthers the University's objective of excellence in research, scholarship,
and education by publishing worldwide in

Oxford   New York

Auckland   Cape Town   Dar es Salaam   Hong Kong   Karachi
Kuala Lumpur   Madrid   Melbourne   Mexico City   Nairobi
New Delhi   Shanghai   Taipei   Toronto

With offices in

Argentina   Austria   Brazil   Chile   Czech Republic   France   Greece
Guatemala   Hungary   Italy   Japan   Poland   Portugal   Singapore
South Korea   Switzerland   Thailand   Turkey   Ukraine   Vietnam

Oxford is a registered trade mark of Oxford University Press
in the UK and in certain other countries

Text and illustrations © Joanne Partis 2005

First published in 2005 as *Sleepytime Kittens*
This edition first published in 2011

British Library Cataloguing in Publication Data
Data available

ISBN: 978-0-19-273162-3 (paperback)

2 4 6 8 10 9 7 5 3 1

Printed in China

Paper used in the production of this book is a natural,
recyclable product made from wood grown in sustainable forests.
The manufacturing process conforms to the environmental
regulations of the country of origin.

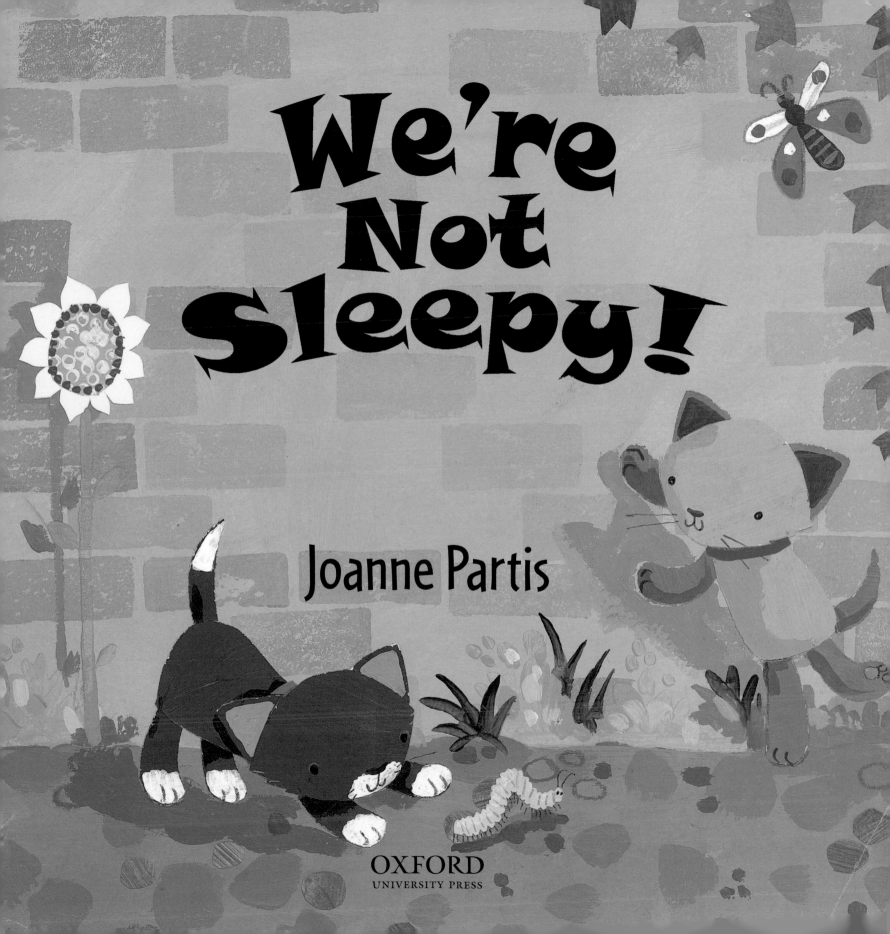

We're Not Sleepy!

Joanne Partis

OXFORD
UNIVERSITY PRESS

It was a warm
summer's evening
down on the farm.

In the farmhouse...

Mum said, 'Time for bed.'
'But we're not sleepy!'
said her three little kittens.

'When you can't sleep, you need
to count sheep,' said Mum.
So the three little kittens set out
to find some sheep to count.

They found . . .

One shaggy sheepdog.

Woof!

But no sheep.

Two munching cows.

Crunch!

Munch! But no sheep.

Three playful foxes.

Jump!
Crash!

Whoops!

But no sheep.

Four bouncy rabbits.

Boing!
Boing!

Boing!
Boing!

But no sheep.

Twit! Twit!

Five hooting owls.

Twit! Twit! Twooooo!

But no sheep.

Six friendly pigs.

Oink! Oink! Oink!

Oink! Oink!
Oink!

But no sheep.

Seven chirping chickens.

Cluck! Cluck!

Cluck!

Cluck! Cluck!

Cluck!

But no sheep.

Quack!

Quack!

Eight noisy ducks.

Quack! Quack!

But no sheep.

Quack!

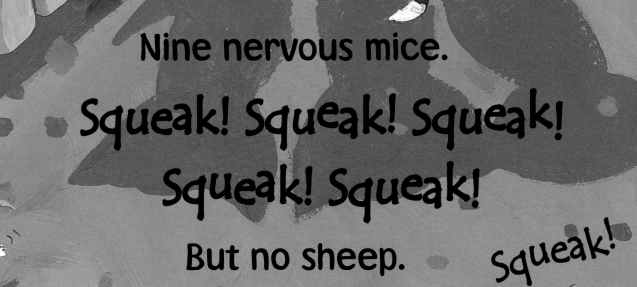

Nine nervous mice.

Squeak! Squeak! Squeak!
Squeak! Squeak!

But no sheep.

Squeak!

Squeak!

Squeak!

By now the kittens had counted
so many things that at last
they felt sleepy.

They stretched,

and yawned,

and snuggled down in the soft grass.
But they weren't the only ones in the field...

Baa! Baa! Baa!

They were
surrounded by
ten surprised
sheep!

Baa!

'I told you it
would work!'

Baa!

I'm on every counting page. Can you find me?

Baa!